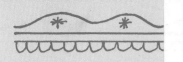

THE PRINCESS
AND THE FROG

Also by A. Vesey
COUSIN BLODWYN'S VISIT
GLORIA

A. VESEY

The Princess and The Frog

Methuen Children's Books · London

For Clemmie, Harry, Flo and George

First published in 1985
by Methuen Children's Books Ltd
11 New Fetter Lane, London EC4P 4EE

Text and illustrations © copyright 1985 by A. Vesey

Printed in Great Britain by
Hazell Watson & Viney Limited,
Member of the BPCC Group,
Aylesbury, Bucks

British Library Cataloguing in Publication Data

Vesey, A.
   The princess and the frog.
   I. Title
   823'.914 [J] PZ7

ISBN 0-416-50300-4

In the Palace gardens, the Princess was playing with her golden ball.

A golden ball does not bounce; all you can do with it
is throw it up and catch it.

The Princess threw it higher and higher. She threw it wildly.
Splash! It fell into the middle of the pond, narrowly missing
a very large frog who was sitting among the lily leaves.
A golden ball does not float; if thrown into a pond it will sink
at once – which is just what this one did.

'Bother,' said the Princess. 'Now I have nothing
to play with.'

'I will fetch your ball for you,' said the frog.
'If in return I may come and live with you
at the Palace. Pond life has its limitations,
and I should like to mix in High Society.'

'All right,' said the Princess, 'if you insist.'
She was anxious to get her ball back.

The frog dived to the bottom of the pond
and brought the golden ball to the Princess.

Then, as it was lunch time, he followed her up the steps to the Palace.

'Mama,' said the Princess to the Queen, 'I lost my
golden ball in the pond, and this frog fetched it
for me. Now he wants to come and live at the Palace.
It is a great nuisance, and he has got very wet feet.'

Now the Queen was considered to be clever.
She took the Princess on one side.

'I know about this,' said the Queen. 'We must
look after the frog and do everything he asks.
One day he will turn into a rich and handsome prince.
You will marry him and live happily ever after.
There are not many rich and handsome princes about;
finding suitable husbands for your six older sisters
has been quite a trial.'

'If you say so, Mama,' said the Princess.

Nothing was too good for the frog.
A beautiful bed was made for him
by the Royal Carpenter.

He had his own special footman
to wait on him hand and foot.

Even the Lord Chamberlain
treated him with the
greatest respect.

Unlike the Princess, who had dull nursery meals
with the Crown Prince, the frog was given
the most delicious things to eat and drink.

'It's not fair,' grumbled the Princess. 'Why can't *I*
have turbot in lobster sauce, Canards à la Rouennaise,
strawberry cream and madeira wine jelly?'

'Eat up your tapioca pudding,' said the frog.

The Princess went to complain to the Queen.

'This frog has been with us for *days*, and there is still no sign of a handsome prince. And besides, he eats too much rich food and is getting fat. I shouldn't care for a fat prince, however rich.'

'Just be patient,' said the Queen. 'These things take time. Meanwhile I shall instruct the Palace Kitchens to put him on a light diet.'

'Hurry up!' called the frog. 'The carriage is waiting; we will be late for the opera.'

The opera lasted for hours, and the frog did not
understand the plot. He slept through most of it,
and snored horribly.

Everywhere the Princess went, the frog went too.

He waved to the crowds from the Royal Carriage.

He went ballooning in the Royal Balloon, and yachting in the Royal Yacht.

He even tried sea bathing, but the salt water got up his nose.

When the Royal Photographer came, the frog sat right in front
of the family group.

Soon everyone at the Palace was tired of the frog.

Archduchess Maud swooned when she found him swimming in her bath.

Miss Grimthorpe, the governess, shuddered at the sight of the frog. He distracted the Princess from her lessons by pulling faces and making rude noises.

The frog's special footman gave notice. The frog gave him so many orders he was suffering from nervous exhaustion.

Monsieur Hollandaise, the Royal Chef, became hysterical. He did not want to make a special light diet for a frog, especially one who stuffed himself with chocolate between meals.

'Mon Dieu!' he snarled, 'if I had my way, frog's legs would be on the menu.'

'This frog must go!' they told the Princess.

The Princess went to complain to the Queen.

'Mama,' said the Princess, 'the frog has been with us for *weeks* and there is still no sign of a handsome prince. Everyone is tired of the frog. He is becoming very grand and bossy. I should not care for a bossy prince, however handsome.'

'Perhaps,' said the King, 'he is not a prince at all, but a reporter from the Daily Record, in pursuit of Royal gossip.'

'Nonsense!' snapped the Queen. 'Just be patient. These things take time.'

Months passed. The Royal Family went on holiday to their castle in the mountains. There was too much walking and climbing for the frog, who did not enjoy exercise. He was relieved when they returned to the Palace.

The Queen summoned the Princess.

'I have just remembered something,' said the Queen. 'To turn the frog into a handsome prince you have to kiss him.'

'KISS THE FROG?' repeated the Princess.

'Yes,' said the queen, 'you must kiss the frog.
Then the spell will be broken and he will be
transformed into the handsomest prince you ever saw.'

'I hope you know what you are talking about,'
said the Princess.

She thought she would get it over with as soon as
possible, so she went to find the frog at once.

'What do you want?' asked the frog, with his mouth full.
He had eaten his light diet and had called for a
more substantial supper before bedtime.

The Princess snatched up the frog. She shut her eyes
tight and kissed him very quickly on the top of his head.
Then she put him down at once.

'Do you mind?' said the frog, 'I am trying to eat my supper. And you can leave out that soppy stuff; I don't like it.'

The Princess opened her eyes. There was no handsome prince. Just a rather fat, bad-tempered frog.

She stamped her foot.

'This is too bad!' said the Princess. 'You come here, pretending to be a handsome prince. You are waited on hand and foot. You eat the most enormous meals. You annoy everyone at the Palace. And then, when I kiss you, what happens? You do not turn into a rich and handsome prince and marry me and take me off to your kingdom. You remain the same disagreeable frog.' She began to cry, more from anger than from anything else.

'I never said I *was* a handsome prince,' said the frog.
'I am a handsome frog. And what is all this fuss about?
You are barely fourteen and much too young to marry anyone.
Besides which, I am not exactly free.'

'Not free?' said the Princess. 'Married, you mean?'

'Yes, married,' said the frog.

'With little frogs?' said the Princess.

'A great many little frogs,' said the frog.

'I wouldn't be in your shoes,' said the Princess. 'You
can't stay here. The Queen will be furious
when she finds out you are not a handsome prince. You
must return to your wife at once. And you had better
think up some very good excuses for staying away so long.
She is not going to be pleased.'

'You could be right about that,' said the frog.
'My wife is quite easily upset. It might be wise
to return to the pond. You had better break the bad news
to the Queen. But first, if you don't mind,
I will get on with my chocolate mousse.'

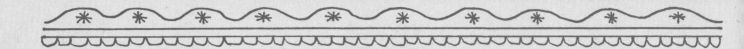